EMMA'S EMU

To Sophia and Nathaniel
—Kenneth Oppel

FIRST FLIGHT® is a registered trademark of Fitzhenry and Whiteside.

Text Copyright © 1999 by Kenneth Oppel
Illustration Copyright © 1999 by Kim LeFave

First published in the United States in 1999.

Fitzhenry & Whiteside acknowledges with thanks the support of the
Government of Canada through its Book Publishing Industry
Development Program in the publication of this title.

Printed in Canada.
Cover and book design by Wycliffe Smith Design.

10 9 8 7 6 5 4 3 2 1

Canadian Cataloguing in Publication Data
Oppel, Kenneth
Emma's emu

(A first flight chapter book)
(A first flight level four reader)
"First flight books"
ISBN 1-55041-524-7

I. LaFave, Kim   II.Series.   III. Series: First flight reader.

PS8579.P64E45 1999a   jC813'.54   C99-931310-X
PZ7.O614Em 1999

A First Flight Level Four Reader

Emma's Emu

Kenneth Oppel
Illustrated by Kim LaFave

Fitzhenry & Whiteside • Toronto

Chapter One

Emma opened the envelope with shaking hands. The letter inside was very short.

Dear Miss Emma Swayne,
Congratulations!
Your grand prize will be arriving
any day!

Emma read the letter again. She could scarcely believe her eyes. She'd actually won something!

For the past two and a half years, Emma had entered every contest she'd come across. She was contest crazy. She filled out entry forms on cereal boxes, bubble gum wrappers and candy bars; she answered skill-testing questions by the hundreds; she hoarded coupons by the thousands. But she'd never won a thing. Not a T-shirt. Not even a paperweight. Not so much as a paperclip.

Until now.

She read the letter once more, just to make sure she'd got it right. Then she rushed upstairs to tell her mother, who was putting the finishing touches on her eye make-up before heading off to work.

"Mom! Look! I've finally won something!"

Mrs. Swayne took the letter and read it carefully.

"Hmmmm," she said.

"I knew it was only a matter of time," said Emma breathlessly.

"Hmmmm," said Mrs. Swayne again. "What's the catch? Do they want you to buy anything?"

"No."

"Do they want you to send money to a

postal box in Zanzibar?"

"No," said Emma impatiently. "I've won. That's all. I've just won!"

"Well," said her mother, "I'll believe it when I see it."

Chapter Two

The very next day, after school, a huge delivery van rumbled to a halt outside Emma's house.

This must be it! Emma thought. This must be my grand prize! Maybe it was the library of astronomy books, or the riding outfit — with six months of free lessons! Maybe it was the Safari holiday, or the hot air balloon!

"This 14 Balmoral Park?" the man asked when she opened the door.

"Yes," she replied.

"Your Mom around?"

"She's still at work."

"Doesn't matter. Sign here."

He handed her a chewed pen and pointed to a spot on the clipboard. Then, over his shoulder, "OK, boys, bring it in."

Two more men jumped out of the cab, and opened the back of the van, hauling out a huge wooden crate.

"Where do you want it, Miss?"

"Um, in the living room, please," said Emma.

They wrestled the crate into the house and dragged it into the middle of the living room.

"OK," said the first man. "We're off."

Emma stood there, staring at the huge crate. What could possibly be inside? Lots of holes were drilled into the wood, but they were too small to see through. Then, from deep inside, came a hollow grunt which sent a shiver through Emma. Whatever's in there, she thought, is definitely alive.

There was a hook at the top of the crate. She nervously pulled it out from the catch, and the front panel fell outwards onto the carpet with a muffled thud. Bits of straw wafted out, along with a thick, spicy smell that was not altogether pleasant.

Then the creature walked out.

Emma took a few steps back.

She supposed it was some sort of bird. But it was certainly unlike any bird she'd ever seen. For starters, it was huge, almost as big as her. It had a dark brown, feathery body, two long and very skinny legs, and a long, snaky neck with a small, beaked head at the end. And as far as Emma could tell, this bird didn't have any wings.

It looked like a feather duster with legs.

The bird swiveled its head round to take in the rest of the living room. Catching sight of the vase of flowers on the coffee table, it made a quick side-step, and devoured the flowers in one hungry bite. The bird looked back at Emma, as if expecting a telling off. Then, with a flamboyant rustling of its feathers, it pooped enthusiastically on the carpet.

"Oh, no!" Emma groaned.

The bird cocked its head, intrigued by the sound of Emma's voice, and made a low, hooting call. Emma jumped. Then the bird set off across the living room at a speedy clip, nibbling a few houseplants as it went. Trailing cautiously behind, Emma was completely at a loss. What was she supposed to do with this strange creature? Probably the best thing would be to get it back into the crate, while she thought things over. But how?

By this time, the bird had reached the bottom of the stairs. It paused, looked upwards pensively, then glanced over to Emma, as if asking a question.

"No, please," she said aloud.

The bird darted up the stairs, two at a time. Emma couldn't believe how fast it was.

"Hey, come back! Come back down here!"

She chased it into her mother's bedroom. It had already hopped up onto the bed and now, with a contented grunt, it dropped its feathery body down onto the duvet.

"Oh no you don't," growled Emma. "You can't nest here! This is Mom's bed!"

The bird just looked at her placidly. Clearly, it didn't care much about Emma's mother.

"Go on! Shoo!" Emma flapped her hands in front of the bird. "Stupid thing!"

In her sudden frustration, Emma

pushed at the creature with all her might.
The bird didn't seem to mind. It just sat
there.

There was obviously no way Emma
could budge it. But she had to get this
thing out of the house before the place
was completely destroyed. She remem-
bered the flowers. This thing liked
flowers. Rushing downstairs, she
snatched some more from the backyard,
leaving the door wide open.

Back in Mom's bedroom, Emma wagged
the tulips in front of the bird's face,
swinging them back and forth like
the pendulum of a grandfather
clock.

The bird grunted, and
perked its neck up, its small
head swaying back and forth
with the flowers.

"Yes, that's right — yum."

Emma started backing out of the
room, dangling the flowers.

The bird hopped off the bed
and started walking cautiously
after her. Emma sped up. So did
the bird. Emma turned and
started running down the

stairs, the bird hard on her heels. She
streaked through the door to the backyard, and hurled the flowers
onto the grass, where they
were quickly devoured.

Emma danced back
inside and slammed the
door shut.

"Ah ha!" she cried
triumphantly. "You're
out, my feathery friend!"

Chapter Three

Emma watched through the window
as the bird strutted around the garden.
It walked eagerly up to a tall bush, disappeared inside, and proceeded to eat it,
leaf by leaf.

"No!" Emma flung open the back door
and raced out. Her mother was going to
be furious!

"Come on, get out of there!" she hissed
into the bushes.

"Hi, what's going on?"

Emma turned and glared. It was
Howie Michinsky. He lived next door,
and was always peering over the garden
wall and striking up conversations with
her. She tried to maneuver herself
between the bird and Howie.

"Nothing's going on, Howie," she said. "Good-bye."

"Oh, I'm not going anywhere," he replied good-naturedly, "I've got lots of time."

A deep, booming call came from the foliage.

"There's something in there!" said Howie in amazement. "Some kind of animal!"

Oh, please, no, thought Emma.

The bird strutted out from the bushes, some leaves still dangling from its beak. It stood there, looking very pleased with itself.

"An emu!" exclaimed Howie.

"A what?" said Emma.

"That's an emu! A flightless bird from Australia! I can't believe it! What's an emu doing here?"

Emma sighed. "I won it."

"You mean in a contest?"

"Uh-huh."

"Wow!" he said enviously, dropping down from the wall and walking closer. "Are you ever lucky!"

"Yeah, some prize," grumbled Emma.

"I was hoping for riding lessons, or a chemistry kit or something. Not some walking dustmop!"

"She's only a baby, really," said Howie. "If she was full grown, she'd be way taller than you."

"How do you know it's a she?"

"Only females make that low, hooting call."

"How come you know all this?" Emma demanded irritably.

"I'm going to be an ornithologist when I grow up," he said solemnly.

"Isn't that like a dentist?"

"That's orthodontist," said Howie. "An ornithologist is someone who studies birds."

"Well, all I know is I've got to hide this thing before Mom gets home."

"Why? Doesn't she like animals?"

"Oh, Mom's not against animals exactly, just so long as they're properly cooked."

Well, she wasn't quite as bad as that, Emma thought. Once, Mrs. Swayne had let Emma have a pet gerbil, but she'd made sure the cage was like a maximum

security prison, with extra-thick bars,
and doors with gerbil-proof locks.

An emu would drive Mrs. Swayne out
of her mind. And Emma could see her
point. This thing was huge. It was smelly.
It pooped on the carpet. No, her mother
would definitely be furious if she came
home to find an emu in the garden.

Worst of all, if her mother found out
she'd won an emu as her grand prize, she
would never, ever, not in a million years,
let Emma enter another contest. That
would be the end of it.

"We could put it in our shed," Howie
suggested. "It's pretty big and we never
use if for anything."

"Good idea," said Emma gratefully.
"Thanks, Howie."

Howie opened the old wooden gate
between their two gardens. The emu high-
tailed it after him, towards the shed.
Emma brought up the rear. Howie opened
the door, and disappeared inside. The
emu hesitated, then followed him. Howie
popped out from around the corner and
slammed the door, fastening it with a loop
of frayed rope.

From inside came a resentful grunt.

"I don't like locking her up," said Emma, "but what else can we do right now?"

"Tomorrow after school, we can let it run around the garden before our parents get back," said Howie.

"OK," said Emma. She looked at her watch and jumped. "Mom'll be home in half an hour, and I've got some serious cleaning up to do. See you later!"

Chapter Four

"There are some good ones over here!" said Howie enthusiastically.

Emma scuttled over on her hands and knees to a rock that Howie had just overturned, revealing a twisting tangle of worms.

"You're sure emus like this sort of thing?" she said, wrinkling her nose.

"Absolutely," said Howie. "I read up on it last night. They eat caterpillars and grasshoppers and stuff. They also like fruit and berries."

Emma brushed her hands and peered critically into the squirming contents of the bucket. "You think we have enough?"

"Maybe."

"OK, let's let her out." She went to

the garden shed, flipped the latch and
pulled back the door. The emu stepped
briskly out, ruffling its feathers indig-
nantly. Howie plonked the bucket down
right in front of it. The emu bent its
head down and took a good look, then
dipped its beak into the bucket and
devoured everything in three seconds.
It looked up expectantly and gave a
scornful grunt.

"She wants more," said Emma.

"So it seems," said Howie.

Emma found some rotten apples, and
Howie yanked up lots of tall grass and
weeds from along the wall.

When the emu was finally
full, Emma and Howie sat
wearily back on the
grass and watched
as it paced the
garden.

"We're going to
run out of food
soon," said
Howie. "The
emu's got a
huge appetite.

It'll gobble up both our gardens in a few days flat!"

"I can't keep it," said Emma. "Mom'll find out sooner or later. Anyway, it's cruel keeping it locked up in the shed." She frowned suddenly. "You know what, Howie? I can't even remember entering any contest for an emu! In fact, I'm sure I didn't. So who gave me this thing?"

"Well," said Howie sensibly, "when they delivered it yesterday, did they give you a receipt?"

Emma sighed. "No. Nothing. How am I supposed to get rid of it?"

"Let's think it over tonight," said Howie. "But right now we'd better get your emu back in the shed before your mom gets home!"

* * *

"Look at this!" Howie told Emma in the playground the next morning. He shoved a newspaper into her hands, tapping at one of the headlines.

NEW EMU FOR LOCAL
SAFARI PARK

The Balmoral Safari Park is expecting the delivery of a rare Australian bird any day now. The female, baby emu is being shipped from a zoo in Sydney, Australia. This will be the second emu to take residence at Balmoral Safari Park. . . .

"We've got their emu!" exclaimed Emma.

"But how did it get delivered to you?" Howie demanded.

Emma quickly read through the rest of the article, and it all clicked into place.

"Look at the park's address!" she said, jabbing her finger at the paper.

"Balmoral Safari Park, 14 Balmoral Park Road," Howie read aloud.

"You see!" exclaimed Emma. "Somehow, the delivery men got the address all mixed up! They delivered it to 14 Balmoral *Park,* my house, instead of 14 Balmoral Park *Road*!"

Howie nodded, impressed. "Well, that solves your problem. Just give them a call and get them to come pick it up."

They ran eagerly to the pay phone at the corner. Emma found the number in the phonebook and punched it in.

"Good morning, Balmoral Safari Park."

"Yes, hello, my name's Emma Swayne, and I'm pretty sure I have your emu."

There was a short pause at the other end.

"Young lady, I really don't have time for this."

"No, please I'm not —"

Emma looked at Howie, incredulous. "She hung up on me! She thought it was all some big joke!"

"There's only one thing left to do," said Howie.

"What?"

"Tell your mom. Maybe they'll listen to a grown-up."

Chapter Five

"She's not home yet," said Emma,
relieved, when she and Howie turned
down their street. "Her car's not there."

She was not looking forward to telling
her mother about the emu.

They turned into Howie's backyard,
and froze in shock. The door to the shed
swung open on its rusty hinges. Emma
ran over and looked inside. Empty.

"Oh no!"

"She must've eaten through the rope,"
said Howie quietly.

"But how'd she get over the walls?"

"I didn't think they could jump that
high," Howie mumbled. "Didn't say
anything about that in my book.

Sorry, Emma."

"It's not your fault, Howie."

They set off along the street right away, peering down people's driveways, peeking into gardens. But there was no sign of the emu.

"Well, cheer up," Howie said to Emma after an hour. "We did our best to find her. At least now you won't have to tell your mom."

"Where were you?" Mrs. Swayne asked when Emma came into the living room. "I was worried."

"Sorry, Mom. I was out playing with Howie."

"By the way, what happened to that grand prize of yours? Has it come yet?"

"Um, no."

"Probably a complete hoax. Never trusted those things."

"Mmmmm," said Emma. She headed to the kitchen for a glass of water, and stopped dead in her tracks. The emu stood silently by the sink, staring at her.

"You rotten, wingless fiend," she growled under her breath. She must have left the back door open earlier, and it had waltzed right back in! Emma spun round on her heel and came back into the living room.

"Mom, can I get you anything from the kitchen? Why don't I make dinner tonight? Here, let me turn on the TV for you."

Mrs. Swayne looked at Emma suspiciously.

"Did you get a detention today or something?" she asked. "Fail a test?"

"No."

"Well, I've already put the dinner on," said Emma's mother, standing. "I should probably check on it."

Emma closed her eyes tight as her mother entered the kitchen. She waited for the scream, but there was only silence. She sighed with relief — the emu must have gone back outside.

Her mother returned to the living room and sat down.

"Sure smells good," said Emma cheerfully.

"I'm sure you don't know anything about that giant bird in our kitchen, do you?"

"Oh, Mom — I can explain!"

"Where did it come from!" exclaimed Mrs. Swayne. She wasn't calm any more. "And what is it doing IN MY HOUSE!"

"There's been a mistake, Mom, a terrible mistake —"

"You won it in a contest, didn't you. I told you those things were no good! I mean, a gerbil's one thing, Emma, but this! You can't keep it, you know! It's not a suitable pet!"

"Mom, please, calm down, I don't want to keep it. It belongs to the safari park, but it got delivered here instead. Honest."

Mrs. Swayne took a deep breath.

"All right. Let's just think about this very calmly." She grabbed the telephone directory and flipped hurriedly through it. "I'm going to call the safari park and get them to pick it up right away."

"I tried that, Mom," said Emma. "They didn't believe me."

"Well, they'll believe me," said Mrs. Swayne determinedly.

Emma waited nervously as her mother dialed the number.

"Yes, good afternoon," she began matter-of-factly. "I have a bird of yours here, an emu." She smiled confidently at Emma. "Yes, of course I can describe it. It's about four feet tall, brown feathers, long neck, skinny legs . . .

no, it doesn't have purple polka dots all over it . . . no, I don't believe in space aliens . . . I am perfectly sane, thank you very much! Now, look —"

Mrs. Swayne blinked in amazement.

"They hung up on me!" she said.

Emma patted her mother reassuringly on the arm. But secretly, she couldn't help feeling a little glad that grown-ups could be as rude to each other as they were to kids.

"Well," said Mrs. Swayne angrily, "we'll just have to take it to the safari park ourselves!"

Chapter Six

Howie had managed to lasso the emu with a long loop of old clothesline, and Emma now pulled gently at the end of the makeshift leash as the huge bird slowly made its way towards the car. Just a few more feet and the emu would be at the wide-open rear door, where Emma had put a particularly succulent piece of watermelon. What emu could resist that?

The emu gazed at the open car door — and the watermelon. Then she looked suspiciously back at Emma.

"What's the problem?" asked Mrs. Swayne impatiently.

"I don't think she wants to go inside," said Howie.

"Can't we just pull her in?" said Mrs.
Swayne.

"We can't force her; it's cruel," said
Emma.

The three of them stood there with
the emu, trying to figure this out. By
now, some of the neighbors were staring
out their windows, or opening their
doors and peering at the spectacle on
Emma Swayne's front lawn.

Then, down the street, a truck
honked: a deep, hooting wail. The emu's
head snapped up, listening. The truck
hooted a second time, and Emma could
feel the huge bird tense against the
clothesline.

Oh, please, she thought. Oh no.

The truck honked once more — and
the emu bolted.

"Hey!"

Holding tight to the clothesline,
Emma was snapped up onto the emu's
shaggy back. She dug her fists into the
dense feathers and hung on for dear life
as the giant bird shot down the street on
its spindly legs.

"Stop!" Emma wailed. "It's just a truck honking!"

But the great bird was unstoppable, convinced it had heard another emu, just down the street.

Holding tight, Emma felt like all her bones were being shaken loose. The emu veered across the pavement, hopped effortlessly over a picket fence, hurtled across someone's garden, then through a back alley.

Jumping a low wall, the emu dashed back out onto the main road.

A car 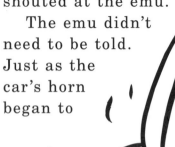 was heading right for them.

"Jump!" Emma shouted at the emu.

The emu didn't need to be told. Just as the car's horn began to

blare, she took a great stride, and leaped high into the air.

"Wow!" shouted Emma, glancing back over her shoulder at the disappearing car. Maybe this emu couldn't fly, but it sure could jump!

By now it was clear to Emma that the emu had no intention of stopping. It was making its bolt for freedom,

and Emma could hardly blame it, it had
been cooped up for so long. At least it
had the sense to stick to the side of the
road. Cars slowly slid past them, the
passengers staring out at them disbe-
lievingly.

"What on earth!" she heard one driver
shout.

"Hey, get that emu off the road!"
another driver bellowed.

They whizzed past a road sign and
Emma made out the words:

BALMORAL PARK ROAD — 2 MILES.

The safari park was on that
road! Suddenly she had an
idea. She managed to
snatch hold of the
dangling clothes-
line around the
great bird's neck.
Then, gathering it
tightly in one

fist, and checking behind her for cars, she tried tugging the line gently to the left.

The emu slowly veered out to the left. Emma pulled the line to the right, and the emu veered back to the right. She could steer! Emma felt pretty pleased with herself. She waited anxiously, until she saw:

> BALMORAL PARK ROAD —
> NEXT RIGHT.

"OK, emu!" she shouted. "We're going this way!"

She pulled firmly on the clothesline and the emu veered neatly round the corner. Emma grinned. By now she was getting used to the emu's humping run. Who needed horse-riding lessons after this!

Behind her she heard the wail of a siren and a police car pulled up alongside. The officer closest to her rolled down the window.

"You can't ride that thing on the road!" the officer shouted through a megaphone. "Pull over immediately!"

"Sorry, Officer!" shouted Emma. "But I can't seem to stop her. I'm trying to steer her towards the safari park."

The officer seemed to consider this.

"All right, then, I'll escort you. Follow me!"

But the emu had different ideas. Before Emma knew what was happening, the emu leaped over the guard rail and hurtled across a field. Cows mooed in consternation.

"What're you doing!" cried Emma. "We were almost there, you dumb bird!"

Emma saw a high chain-link fence in
the distance. Soon she could make out a
big sign. NO TRESPASSING, it said,
and underneath, in smaller letters:
BALMORAL SAFARI PARK.

Well, thought Emma, we made it after
all. Now we've just got to find the back
door!

This, however, was not what the emu
had in mind. The huge bird speeded up,
heading straight for the fence.

"Stop!" Emma shouted, yanking on
the clothesline. "It's too high!"

She was so frightened she didn't even
clamp her eyes shut. The emu launched
itself off the ground and sailed up into
the air. It soared high, just clearing
the top of the fence,

then plummeted back down on the other side.

At last the emu came to a standstill. They were in a vast field of tall yellow grass. It was very still and hot, with only the droning of insects in the air. Emma felt like she was in a different country. It looked like one of those nature documentaries on TV.

"Well, thank goodness that's over with!" She started to swing her aching leg over the emu's back when a flash of movement caught her eye. Her whole body clenched with fear.

A lion stalked through the tall grass towards them.

"Giddyap!" Emma shouted, knocking her ankles against the emu's sides. "Come on, emu! No time to relax now!"

The emu's sharp eyes had already spotted the lion, and it bolted, almost throwing Emma off its back. With an ear-splitting roar, the lion lunged, its outstretched claws falling mere inches from the emu's legs.

Emma looked back and saw the lion plunging after them. This is it, she thought. Girl Eaten by Lion in Safari Park. But the emu had no intention of giving up. It raced on across the hot grassy plain, and then, with a great stride, made a flying leap and landed with a splash in the middle of a swampy river.

The lion hung back, pacing furiously on the shore.

Scaredy cat! thought Emma. Doesn't want to get its fur wet!

The emu paddled along through the murky river. Emma's legs were getting soaked, right up to her knees, but she didn't mind. She was so relieved to be clear of that lion.

"Pretty smart for a wingless bird, aren't you," said Emma, patting the emu on the back.

The bird just made one of its noncommittal grunts.

But a few seconds later Emma realized why the lion stayed out of the water. A long, knobby green shape was gliding towards them, with two malevolent green eyes bulging above the surface. Huge jaws snapped open, exposing the crocodile's deep, jagged rows of teeth.

The emu paddled furiously, making for the shore. But it was no match for the crocodile, slithering fast through the water. Emma knew she was slowing the emu down! She looked desperately in all directions, then saw the approaching trees, branches hanging far out over the water, drooping moss-covered vines.

Emma stood up on the emu's back, arms outstretched for balance. She could see the crocodile, its jaws almost at the emu's tail feathers.

She jumped, grabbed for one of the hanging vines, and went swinging forwards. The emu, with a new burst of speed, surged into the shallows, and up onto dry land, leaving the crocodile thrashing angrily in the water. Emma swung in close to shore, saw another vine ahead of her and instinctively grabbed it. Then, with a sharp snap, the vine broke!

Emma landed with a soft thud right on the emu's back.

"Nice timing," she gasped, patting its neck.

The emu loped on tiredly through the trees until it came out onto another open field. It looked around, and, with a grunt, dropped its body onto the grass.

The sound of a car motor made Emma look up, shading her eyes against the sun. A jeep came towards her, driven by a man in a pale, wide-brimmed hat.

"What on earth is going on!" he cried, jumping out, and walking quickly towards Emma and her emu.

"My name's Emma Swayne," she told
the man, "and this, I believe, is your
emu."

"Our emu? But how?"

She calmly explained the whole thing,
while he listened with wide eyes, shaking his head in amazement.

"Incredible!" he said. "My name's
Jack Havanna. I'm the park warden."

"Pleased to meet you," said Emma.
She finally swung herself off the emu.
When her feet touched ground, she
almost toppled over. Her legs felt like
liquorice sticks.

Another jeep roared up, and this time
Emma's mother and Howie jumped out,
along with an assistant gamekeeper.

Mrs. Swayne ran up to Emma and
hugged her close. "Are you all right?"
she said.

"Yes, fine," said Emma.

"You rode the emu!" said Howie in awe.

"I was getting pretty good at it, too."

"You, Emma Swayne, are a very brave
girl," Jack Havanna told her. "And I'm
extremely grateful to you for bringing us
our emu. Before you go, I'd like to give

you a year-round pass for you and as many guests as you like."

"Really?" said Emma.

"You can come to the park whenever you want, and visit the emu. Of course, it's probably a good idea if you don't ride the emu again."

Emma laughed. "OK, I promise."

From the distance came a familiar hooting call, and Emma watched as her emu perked up, stood quickly, and ran after it.

"We have another emu here, a male," said Mr. Havanna. "Yours was meant to be its mate."

As they all rode back across the field in the warden's jeep, Emma saw the two emus together in the distance, grazing happily in the tall grass.

***

Back home, Emma and Howie sat in the living room, drinking lemonade.

"Wow, a year-round pass to the safari park," said Howie enviously. "Lucky you."

"Lucky you, too," said Emma with a smile. "You can come with me whenever you want."

"Honest?"

"Of course, Howie."

Howie broke into a huge grin. "They've got all these rare, tropical birds there — toucans and ostriches and African falcons! It's way better than looking at pictures in books!"

"You know what, though," said Emma suddenly. "I never did get that grand prize!"

In all the excitement and confusion of getting the emu back to the safari park, she'd completely forgotten about the mysterious letter, telling her about the prize which would be arriving any day.

"Well, it doesn't really matter," she said cheerfully. After all, she thought to herself, she'd ended up with an emu, an adventure and maybe best of all, a good friend.

She was just pouring herself another glass of lemonade when she heard a horn honking outside her house.

"What's that?" said Mrs. Swayne, coming into the room.

Frowning, Emma went to the window. A huge truck had pulled up outside. A man was coming towards the door, slapping a clipboard against his leg.

"Oh-oh," said Howie.

"Oh no!" said Mrs. Swayne.

"Finally!" exclaimed Emma, running for the door.

FIRST FLIGHT®

*FIRST FLIGHT® is an exciting
new series of beginning readers.
The series presents titles which include songs,
poems, adventures, mysteries, and humour
by established authors and illustrators.
FIRST FLIGHT® makes the introduction to
reading fun and satisfying
for the young reader.*

*FIRST FLIGHT® is available in 4 levels
to correspond to reading development.*

Level 1 – Pre-school - Grade 1
Large type, repetition of simple concepts that are perfect
for reading aloud, easy vocabulary and endearing
characters in short simple stories for the earliest reader.

Level 2 – Grade 1 - Grade 3
Longer sentences, higher level of vocabulary, repetition,
and high-interest stories for the progressing reader.

Level 3 – Grade 2 - Grade 4
Simple stories with more involved plots and a simple
chapter format for the newly independent reader.

Level 4 – Grade 3 - up (First Flight Chapter Books)
More challenging level, minimal illustrations for the
independent reader.